Paul Rogers

Sheepchase

Illustrated by
Celia Berridge

PUFFIN BOOKS

Wake up Jack, you sleepyhead!
Or you'll lose a sheep.
Flossie thinks: "That fair looks fun!
I'll go, while Jack's asleep."

"Asleep again!" the farmer shouts,
"And Flossie's missing too!
Find her quick! Where did she go?"
Jack doesn't know. Do you?

He finds her footprints on the track
Leading to the mill.
But which way has Flossie gone,
Up or down the hill?

"Sorry Jack," the miller says,
"There are no sheep about.
There's nothing here but heaps of flour."
But what's that peeping out?

Flossie makes a run for it.
"After her!" they roar.
Is she going to cross the bridge?
What's she stopping for?

All at once they hear a splash.
Is Flossie trying to swim?
But then they see the fisherman –
What's Flossie done to *him*?

There's the boat beside the steps.
"Missed her again," they sigh.
"But someone, somewhere must have seen
A stray sheep trotting by."

There's trouble in the market place.
Jack runs ahead to see.
Something must have made them shout –
Whatever can it be?

Round the corner, down the street
Leading to the fair:
This is the way that Flossie went.
She's here for sure – but where?

"Balloons for sale!" the pedlar shouts
"Roll up! The fair's in town!"
Flossie darts between his legs
And nearly knocks him down.

Where should they begin to look?
Jack has no idea.
"Hurrah! I've made it!" Flossie thinks.
"I'll have a good time here!"

"*Now* which way?" they ask themselves.
"She must have got away."
No one sees her take a leap
Into a pile of hay.

"What's the use?" the farmer sighs
"Back to the flock! Go on!"
She could be miles away by now.
Who knows where Flossie's gone?

"What a day! I'll count the sheep
And then I'll sleep," thinks Jack.
Then suddenly he hears a Baaaaah!
Look – Flossie's back!

For Emma P.R.